ZOO RESCUE

by

JANE A.C. WEST AND ROGER HURN

Illustrated by Stik

Tribe
Book 4

To John and Pip

With special thanks to:

Wa'fy Abdullah
Alfie Blair
Emma Crane
Annabel Dannheim
Elizabeth Duffy
Luc Issolah
Annalee Mullins
Max Murphy
Samuel Spring
Alejandro Stone
Oliver Stuart
Thomas Ward

First published in 2011 in Great Britain by
Barrington Stoke Ltd
18 Walker St, Edinburgh, EH3 7LP

www.barringtonstoke.co.uk

ISBN: 978-1-84299-602-7

Printed in China by Leo

The publisher gratefully acknowledges support from the Scottish Arts
Council towards the publication of this title.

Scottish
Arts Council

WHO ARE TRIBE?

ARE THEY HUMANS?

OR ARE THEY ANIMALS?

Tribe are humans *and* animals.

They are super-heroes with special powers.

They can *shape-shift* – change from animals to humans and back again.

THEIR PLAN: to save the world from anyone who tries to destroy it.

Tribe need to find the bad guys – before it's too late.

The Earth is in trouble – and only Tribe have the power to help.

Tribe are helped by TOK – the Tree Of Knowledge.

Tribe can travel all over the world using the roots of trees.

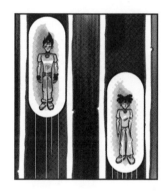

Tribe also have the power to talk to animals – and they can send each other mind-messages, even when they are miles apart.

CAST LIST

Finn

Bruin

Kat

Mo

Talon

Vana

and ...

Yu See-Mee!

Contents

Chapter 1
Bearing Bad News

Tribe were in their Head Quarters in the Tree Of Knowledge (TOK). A message flashed up on the Sap Screen.

"What's up, Bruin? You've got a face like a wet weekend," said Vana.

1

"He always looks like that!" smiled Finn.

"Grr!" said Bruin. "This is really bad news. A Giant Panda has been put in a zoo in China."

"Don't they do that to protect them?" said Finn.

"Would *you* like to be put in a cage?" growled Bruin. "This panda is not just any Giant Panda – it's my friend, Po Po." Bruin was upset and angry.

"What do you want to do?" asked Vana.

"Set him free!" said Bruin.

"I'll call the rest of Tribe," said Vana.

e sent a mind-message to call everyone to the tree-house. It was one of Tribe's special powers – it was a way of talking to each other without words.

Vana told them what had happened to Po Po. Then they jumped into a tree trunk. The root system went everywhere in the world that had trees. Now they were going to China set Po Po free.

Chapter 2
The Zoo in China

Tribe came out of a tree trunk near Lanzhou airport in China. The air was sizzling hot – and very polluted. It was so thick and murky that they couldn't see the circle of mountains round the city.

"Yuk! How do people breathe this air?"

sniffed Kat.

"If they planted more trees it would make the air cleaner," whispered Mo.

"They would have to plant lots and lots of trees to clear up this mess," said Talon.

"Let's get to the zoo," said Bruin.

Someone had tried hard to make the zoo look nice. Trees stood at the entrance and a man was washing the dust and dirt off their leaves with a hose-pipe.

"People do care about this place,"
whispered Mo, "but it's still a prison for
animals."

The animals watched Tribe from their
cages. Chinese Leopards swished their long
tails and growled.

Two snub-nosed monkeys pointed the
way to the panda cage.

"Bruin, look!" Mo tugged on Bruin's
sleeve. "There he is!"

The Giant Panda was sitting in his cage with his back to the visitors, who were shouting at him and trying to get him to turn round. But Po Po just sat there, gazing at the concrete floor of his cage.

"Get rid of these visitors!" whispered
Bruin.

Vana morphed into a wolf. Kat winked at
Vana, then screamed, "Aaaaagh! It's a wolf!
She's got out of her cage! Help! Help!"

Vana trotted off, with a wolfish grin, as the frightened visitors ran for their lives.

"Hey, brother," whispered Bruin. "Po Po, it's me."

Chapter 3
The Cage

Po Po stood up. He wrapped his huge paws around the bars of his cage and his sad eyes gazed at Bruin.

"I had a dream you would come for me. Are you real?"

"As real as you, brother," said Bruin.
"Don't worry. We'll get you out of here."

"How?" cried Po Po. "My cage is made of concrete and iron. How can you get me out?"

"We'll think of something. How did they catch you?"

"Men came," said Po Po. "They said I was eating their crops and stealing their food. It was a lie. Everyone knows pandas eat bamboo."

Vana ran back to them in her human form.

"We've got the key to Po Po's cage!" she said. "Mo took it from the zoo keeper when he was busy chasing an angry wolf."

"You've got a terrible temper, haven't you, Vana?" grinned Talon.

Vana looked at Po Po.

"We'll come back at night when the zoo is closed," said Vana. "We'll get you out then, Po Po."

"Thank you!" said Po Po. "Look out for the head zoo keeper, Yu See-Mee. He's as mean as a cat with tooth-ache ... er ... no offence," said Po Po, looking at Kat.

"None taken," said Kat with a flash of her green eyes.

"The other keepers are nice, but he's mean. He doesn't like animals. He hits us when no one is looking. If we don't do tricks for the visitors, he doesn't feed us."

"He's toast!" yelled Finn. "We have to stop him. Let's let all the animals out."

"I was thinking about that," said Vana. "We can get Po Po to the mountains outside the city, but none of the other animals could survive there. They'd starve to death. We'll have to leave them here. Don't worry, Finn. We'll make sure the evil zoo-keeper Yu See-Mee is stopped for good. Then it will be a better zoo. Leave it to me."

"What are you planning?" said Kat.

Vana smiled. "Wait and see!"

Chapter 4
Mo's Silly Idea

Even at night the zoo was never silent. The elephants called to each other and the lions roared their rage at the starry sky.

Tribe were hiding in the bushes near the zoo. "How long do we have to hide in these bushes?" asked Finn.

"Hush!" whispered Vana. "Mo – go and

have a look. Let us know if it's safe for us to

come out."

Mo morphed into a mouse and scampered to the zoo's entrance. She was back in a moment.

"Yu See-Mee is there. He'll see anyone going in and out."

"It sounds like a job for me," said Talon. "I'll fly in with the key and let Po Po out."

"But how are we going to get a Giant Panda across the city without anyone seeing him?" asked Kat.

"I've got an idea," said Mo. "It's a bit silly, but it could work … It's the Chinese Lantern Festival tonight and there's going to be a parade passing by the zoo. All the children make lanterns in the shapes of different animals. And they always have people dressed up as Chinese dragons.

We could hide Po Po under a Chinese dragon costume! Then we can all join the parade and Po Po can escape."

Vana smiled. "That's brilliant, Mo! And it'll be fun, too. Let's go!"

Tribe had to work fast. There wasn't much time.

Chapter 5
Kung Fu Panda

Bruin, Kat and Finn ran to a fancy dress shop and got a Chinese dragon costume. Bruin put on the huge dragon's head. The others made up the body and tail. They were hidden under sheets of yellow silk. They had to hurry – the parade had already begun.

"Ouch! Watch where you're going!" hissed Kat, when Finn trod on her toe.

"Sorry," said Finn. "I can't see a thing under here. I could do with cats' eyes."

"Shut up!" said Bruin. "We're almost at the zoo."

Yu See-Mee left his office and went to watch the parade march past the zoo gates.

29

Vana morphed into a wolf and charged at Yu See-Mee, showing her fangs. The evil zoo keeper ran away screaming for help – but no one could hear him because of the noise of the parade. Vana chased him, snapping at his heels.

Talon and Mo ran to Po Po's cage.

"Quick!" said Bruin as Talon led Po Po out of the zoo. "Hide under the dragon costume."

"Let's get going," said Finn.

Hidden under the dragon costume, they joined the parade and marched down the street.

"I know," said Finn, "Let's show them a real Kung Fu Panda!"

They began to do a Kung Fu dragon dance and the crowd cheered. With all the noise and fun going on no one noticed that four of the dragon's feet were covered in thick, black panda fur.

Chapter 6
Mountain Home

As the parade marched down the street, the bright yellow Chinese dragon turned down a side street and hurried off.

"It's hot in here," said Finn as he pulled off the yellow silk cloth.

"My hair is a mess," said Kat crossly.

"Yeah," said Finn. "The fur has been flying."

Vana gave them a cross look.

"Thank you, brothers. Thank you, sisters," said Po Po. "I am free. Now I can go back to the mountains. This time I will climb higher, far away from people."

Together Tribe and Po Po went higher and higher into the mountains, taking Po Po to his new home.

"Stay safe, brother," said Bruin. "I'll come back and see you when you've found your new home and settled in. I can help you hunt some bamboo."

"You will be very welcome, brother," smiled Po Po, "even if bamboo doesn't run very fast."

"By the way, Vana," said Bruin. "What did you do with that evil zoo keeper?"

"Oh, him!" said Vana, with a chuckle. "I chased him into the lion's cage."

"You didn't leave him there, did you?" squeaked Mo.

"Yes, I did leave him there," said Vana. "He was trying to climb a tree when I left.

Don't worry. I had a word with the lions.
I told them to give him a good fright but not
to eat him. He'd be too tough. And then I
talked to the local newspaper and told them
that Yu See-Mee is mean to the zoo animals.
They'll have a photographer there first thing
in the morning."

"That's brilliant!" said Talon.

"Yeah, you were *fang*-tastic!" grinned
Finn.

GIANT PANDAS ALMOST EXTINCT

There are only a few Giant Pandas left in the world. Fewer than 3,000 pandas live in the wild.

Farming, pollution, new towns and hunting have almost wiped them out. Pandas prefer to live in the low-lands. Humans have forced them to live high up in the mountains of China.

For many years zoos have kept Giant Pandas to make sure they didn't become extinct. Some zoos do an important job in keeping rare animals alive, but not many Giant Pandas are born in zoos. They just aren't happy having cubs in a zoo.

In the wild Giant Pandas roam large areas looking for food. In zoos they have plenty of food and medicine and are safe from hunters – but they don't have much space. In the wild they might live between 15 and 20 years. In a zoo they can live up to 35 years.

BRUIN - BEAR BOY

THE JOKER. ALWAYS UP FOR A LAUGH BUT STRONG AND STEADY WHEN THE JOKES ARE OVER.

SPECIAL SKILL: very strong.

LOVES: walking in the woods.

HATES: small spaces, bear baiting, zoos.

MOST LIKELY TO SAY: "You're having a laugh!"

BIGGEST SECRET: has bad dreams about his long lost parents.

TRIBE TALK!

To:	Bruin
From:	Jake
Subject:	Zoos

Dear Bruin,

My grandma wants to take me and my little brother to the zoo. I think keeping animals in cages is cruel. What can I do?

Jake

To:	Jake
From:	Bruin
Subject:	Re: Zoos

Hi Jake,

I know how you feel. None of us like seeing animals in cages. But don't forget that zoos do important work too to make sure animals do not die out. And they're a way for people to learn about animals and their habitats..

Make sure the zoo you're going to visit is one of the good ones. You can check it out at www.goodzoos.com. Or ask your gran if you can visit a safari park instead. These outdoor animal parks try to copy an animal's wild habitat. Check out www.safaripark.co.uk. If you're worried about the well-being of any animal, contact the Royal Society for the Prevention of Cruelty to Animals www.rspca.org.uk.

Paws for applause,

Bruin.

TURN THE PAGE
FOR MORE
FUN STUFF!

FYI: GIANT PANDAS

 • They may look cuddly, but they've still got claws!

 • The Giant Panda is a bear.

 • They don't eat much meat. They like to eat bamboo, honey, eggs, oranges and bananas.

• Giant Pandas are only found wild in China.

 • When born, a baby Giant Panda weighs as little as 100g. As adults they can weigh 150kg!

 • A panda's front paws have four fingers and a thumb – just like us.

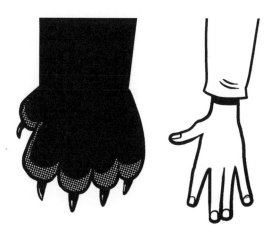

JOKE OF THE DAY

BRUIN: Why do bears have fur coats?

FINN: I don't know...

BRUIN: Because they look silly in anoraks!

CHECK OUT THE REST OF
THE TRIBE BOOKS!

For more info check out our website:
www.barringtonstoke.co.uk